Alone in the Night

Alone in the Night

by Holly Webb

Illustrated by Sophy Williams

tiger tales

tiger tales

5 River Road, Suite 128, Wilton, CT 06897
Published in the United States 2017
Originally published in Great Britain 2009
by the Little Tiger Group
Text copyright © 2009 Holly Webb
Illustrations copyright © 2009 Sophy Williams
ISBN-13: 978-1-68010-409-7
ISBN-10: 1-68010-409-8
Printed in China
STP/1800/0127/0317
10 9 8 7 6 5 4 3 2 1

For more insight and activities, visit us at www.tigertalesbooks.com

Contents

For Tom

Chapter One
Star's Outdoor Adventure

"Jasmine! Hurry up! You're going to be late for school!" Jasmine's mom glanced at her watch—and then at all the other children wearing the same uniform as her daughter, who were streaming past the end of their street.

Jasmine looked up. "Oh, but I was just saying hello to Tiger, Mom!" The marmalade tabby cat sitting on the wall ducked his head so Jasmine could rub his ears. Then he stood up and leaned over to bump the side of his head against her chin. Jasmine had read so many books about cats and knew that he wasn't just being cute. He was rubbing his scent glands on her. It was pretty cute, too, though. All the cats in the street loved Jasmine—which is why it always took her so long to get to school.

"Jasmine, we left the house 10 minutes ago and we haven't even gotten past next door!" Her mom sighed. "You're going to be late."

"I'm sorry, Mom." Jasmine smiled at her apologetically. "Let's run!"

She was just picking up her school bag when she stopped again. "Oh, Mom, look! In the window next door!"

She pointed across the yard.

"Oh, a kitten."

"Mom! A beautiful kitten! I haven't seen her before. Did you know the new people next door had a kitten?"

The kitten was tiny, perched right in the middle of the big windowsill, which made her look even tinier. Jasmine could just about make out her beautiful stripy brown tabby markings.

"No, I didn't," Mom said, leading her away. Jasmine walked backward, still staring at the kitten, who stared back. "You know we haven't really said any more than a quick hello while they were unpacking."

"Poor little kitten. They must have left her all alone while they've gone to work," Jasmine said sadly.

"Oh, Jasmine! Cats don't mind being on their own," her mom laughed. "Besides, how do you even know that kitten's a she? It could be a boy."

"She just looked like a she," Jasmine said. "And cats do get lonely, Mom, especially when they're only babies."

"I'm sure they'll play with her when they get home," Mom comforted her. "Now run!"

Jasmine turned out to be right—the kitten was a girl. Her mom invited Helen, the new lady next door, to come over for coffee and found out all about her beautiful cat.

"Her name is Star," Jasmine told her best friend, Laura, as they walked home from school together. "She's got such cute tabby stripes; she's really beautiful." Jasmine sighed. "She looks exactly like my dream cat—you know, the one I'd really like to have for my own someday."

"Oh, you're so lucky having her next door. She might come into your yard," Laura said enviously. "Do you know how old she is?"

"Almost three months. She was given to them by a friend whose cat had kittens. They were a bit worried she'd be upset by the move, but she doesn't mind. Except she's desperate to go out!"

"Can't they let her out?" Laura asked.

"Not until she's had all her vaccinations in a couple of weeks," Jasmine explained. "See you tomorrow!" she called as they got to her gate.

During the next few weeks, Jasmine watched for Star every time she walked past the house next door and always waved hello. Sometimes, if she was sitting on the windowsill, the little cat would stand up on her back legs and scratch hopefully at the glass with her paws, as though she hoped she might be able to slip through and come out for Jasmine to pet her. Jasmine wished she could, too.

Star finished washing herself and looked thoughtfully around the yard. She still wasn't very used to being outside. In fact, today was the first day that her owners had left her in the house with the cat flap unlocked. She'd been allowed out all on her own a few times over the weekend, and they'd put out big bowls of cat snacks to make sure she came back. Of course she had! She loved her house, and her basket, and her food bowls, and her people. She just wanted to explore what was outside.

She headed to the end of the yard. The bushes there were fascinating, full of nests and tunnels and places to hide. When she'd finished investigating and wriggled out again, her eyes were sparkling with excitement. She licked the fur around her mouth thoughtfully, trying to get rid of the rather strange taste of beetle. Beetles looked delicious, like walking cat snacks, but they didn't taste good.

Star sat down in the middle of the lawn, closing her eyes for a moment and feeling the warm autumn sunshine on her fur. Then she went and rolled around in a pile of dried leaves. When she'd gotten bored of that game, she stretched out her front paws and then her back paws, looking for something to do next. There was a snail moving very slowly along a leaf just next to her, and she watched that for a little while, but she'd learned from the beetle and didn't try to eat it.

That was when she spotted the gap under the fence. Star didn't really know what the fence was. She didn't quite understand that there was a whole new yard on the other side of it. But she knew that the little hole looked interesting.

The gap wasn't very big, and she had to scratch a little at the earth underneath to get through. Star still had little soft indoor kitten paws, with apricot-pink pads, and digging her way under the fence rubbed off a little of their newness. It felt good.

She emerged in the yard next door and gave herself a quick wash. Then she looked around with interest.

Suddenly she caught sight of Jasmine. Her eyes widened—Jasmine was so quiet that she'd thought she was alone. But she didn't dive back under the fence. Star recognized the girl—she was the friendly one who always waved when she walked past the house.

It was the middle of the fall break. Jasmine was in the yard putting out the leftover toast crusts from breakfast on the bird feeder when she caught a little grayish-brown flash in the corner of her eye. She turned her head slowly, hoping to see what kind of bird it was. But it wasn't a sparrow hopping around in the bushes. It was a cat.

Not just any cat.... *The* cat. It was little Star from next door.

She was squeezing herself under the fence, wriggling and scrambling, with such a determined expression on her face that Jasmine had to bite her lip to stop herself from giggling—she didn't want to scare Star away.

The kitten finally popped out from under the fence like she'd been pushed and twitched her tail angrily. Then she sat down to wash herself, brushing her paw thoroughly around her ears in case she'd gotten them grubby fighting her way through.

Jasmine perched on the bench and watched her, not even wanting to breathe too deeply in case she frightened the tiny creature. She'd been hoping to meet Star for so long, and the kitten was only a few feet away.

Now Star had obviously seen her. She stood up daintily and padded over to Jasmine. No one had petted her since Helen and Andy left for work, and even though exploring was fun, she wanted someone to pay attention to her. She stopped a little ways away, just far enough to make a run for it if Jasmine turned out not to be friendly, and gave a hopeful little meow.

Jasmine reached out her hand slowly. She couldn't believe Star had come this close—she'd thought that such a little kitten would be too nervous. She could almost touch Star's nose, but she didn't. She just held out her fingers, and whispered, "Here, kitty, hello Star...."

Star's ears pricked slightly. The girl knew her name! That had to be good.

She pranced a few steps closer and rubbed her head affectionately against Jasmine's leg.

Jasmine laughed and petted Star's ears, and Star made a big leap and sprang onto the bench next to her, then climbed into Jasmine's lap. There she gave a contented little sigh and closed her eyes, massaging Jasmine's jeans with her little needle-sharp claws. Good. Proper petting.

Jasmine smiled down at her, wishing she had a beautiful kitten of her very own. It was such a shame that her mom and dad weren't really pet people. But maybe beautiful little Star could help convince them....

From then on, Jasmine always looked for Star in the yard, and Star soon figured out what time Jasmine got home from school. If she was bored, or wanted someone to play with, she would wriggle under the fence— she'd had to make the hole quite a lot bigger by now—and jump from the bench onto the kitchen windowsill. Then she would meow plaintively for

Jasmine to come out and see her.

Jasmine's mom thought it was funny at first, but then she got a little worried. What if the next-door neighbors didn't like Jasmine spending all this time with their kitten?

One day the kitchen window was open—Jasmine's mom had been cooking chili for dinner and wanted to let the smell out—and when Jasmine came into the kitchen, she saw Star nosing curiously around the gap, obviously wondering if she was allowed to step in through the window.

Jasmine didn't even think. She just held out her hand and made little noises to Star, tempting her in. She couldn't imagine anything nicer than cuddling

Star in her own kitchen. Unless it was in her bedroom, of course….

Jasmine's mom was horrified when she came up to see how Jasmine was doing with her homework. "Jasmine! What's that cat doing in here?" she cried.

Star gave a nervous little squeak and disappeared off Jasmine's lap under the desk.

Jasmine glared at her mom and crouched down to try and coax the kitten out. "You frightened her!"

"She frightened me!" her mom retorted. "She's not supposed to be in our house, Jasmine. She's the next-door neighbors' cat!"

"I bet they wouldn't mind," Jasmine muttered. She knew she shouldn't really have let Star in, but she'd been so lonely, meowing on the windowsill. "They don't get home until later, Mom; she just wanted a hug!"

"Jasmine, she's not ours. She'll end up getting confused about where she

lives—she's only little. Put her outside!"
her mom said firmly. And Jasmine had
to gather up Star and take her back
downstairs.

"I'm sorry, Star!" Jasmine muttered
as she slipped the kitten out the back
door. Her mom was watching, her arms
folded sternly, and Jasmine knew she'd
be pushing her luck if she went outside,
too. But it was getting dark and had
started to rain. She felt so guilty putting
Star out in the cold, wet yard.

Star watched the door close, looking
up at it sadly. Why hadn't Jasmine's
mother wanted her? She didn't
understand. She shook her whiskers,
feeling confused, then slunk across the
yard, under the fence, and back through
her cat flap.

Chapter Two
Locked Out!

After Mom had made her take Star
outside, Jasmine didn't risk letting her
in the house again, no matter how much
she wanted to. For the next few weeks,
she played with Star in the yard instead,
even though it was November and
freezing cold. Star's beautiful fur coat
kept her a lot warmer than Jasmine's
blue school jacket, but she didn't want

to miss out on playing with the kitten.

"Jasmine! Come on in. It's snack time!" Jasmine's mom called from the back door.

Jasmine picked up Star and put her gently on top of the fence—she liked jumping onto it now that she was a little bigger, instead of scrambling underneath. "Bye, Star! See you tomorrow," she said, petting the little cat's nose. Star was in that funny stage now where she was half-kitten, half-cat, and all legs.

Her mom was still looking out the back door. "Aren't you frozen? Look, your hands are bright red; where are your gloves?"

Jasmine wiggled her fingers, which were feeling very numb now. "I was petting Star. You can't pet a cat with gloves on, Mom."

Her mom shook her head, smiling. "You and that cat."

Star jumped lightly down from the wall and trotted back to her cat flap. She was very cold, and she wanted to go inside. But when she nudged her cat flap with her nose, it didn't open. Star butted it harder, but she only hurt her nose. She meowed angrily. Then she tried scratching at the cat flap, but that didn't work, either. The flap was stuck, and it wouldn't budge.

Star meowed again, louder this time, hoping her owners would hear. But no one came. Miserably, she crept away and hid under a bush close to the door, waiting for the house lights to come on to show that her owners were home.

It seemed as though she waited forever, while the yard grew darker and darker, and more cold. Even her tail ached with it. It was too cold to sleep, and she was so hungry. She got up and went to stare sadly through the cat flap at her food bowl. Usually her owners would be home by now, she was sure. Where were they? Star didn't like being on her own. She liked people, and being petted. She looked back across the dark yard to Jasmine's house. If only she could go inside. It would be so nice and warm in there.

Suddenly, the fur on her back rose up

as she sensed that another cat was in her yard, and not one she liked. She'd met quite a few other cats during the last few weeks. Some had been friendly, and some had warned her away. She jumped around, whiskers bristling, and saw an enormous dark shape creeping toward her. A dark shape that hissed.

Star squeaked with fright and backed up against the wall, darting a quick, desperate glance at her cat flap. But it was still shut tight.

The black cat padded closer and hissed again, and then swiped at her with one huge dark paw, sending her skidding away.

Star skittered across the yard and dived for the hole under the fence. Frantically, she squeezed her way through, even though it was much too tight, and shot out into Jasmine's yard. At least the hole was too small for that huge black cat to follow her. Star ran over to Jasmine's back door and let out a panicky howl, hoping Jasmine would come and rescue her.

She'd been right. The hole was too

small for the black cat. But she could hear him scrambling up the fence....

Jasmine was asleep, dreaming of a horrible spelling test, when her teacher suddenly turned into a meowing cat. She wriggled and turned over, muttering in her sleep. But the meowing didn't stop, and eventually she woke up, blinking worriedly into the darkness. That was Star!

Jasmine hopped out of bed and pulled on her robe. She was leaning over the top of the stairs when her dad came out of the living room.

"Oh, did they wake you, Jasmine? Don't be scared; it's just some cats fighting in the yard. I'm going to chase them away."

Jasmine shook her head anxiously and ran down the stairs toward him. "No, Dad, don't! That sounds like Star, the kitten from next door. I'm sure she's not fighting. She's really scared, I can tell."

Her dad sighed. "Your mom said you'd fallen in love with that cat. Come on, then, let's see what's going on."

He opened the back door, and there on the step, shivering, was a tiny little tabby, her fur all up on end and her tail looking like a feather duster. Lurking a couple of feet away, its eyes shining green in the light from the kitchen, was the biggest black cat Jasmine had ever seen.

"Oh! It's Sam, from down the road. He's always fighting. He has only half an ear, and Mrs. James has to take him to the vet about once a month. We can't let him fight with Star; he's so huge that he'd just squash her!" Jasmine went out onto the step, not caring about her bare feet. "Shoo, Sam! Go home, bad cat!"

Sam backed off, but only a little ways. Star gave a miserable little meow, and Jasmine picked her up gently. "Dad, please can we bring her inside? I know the Murrays wouldn't mind, not if she was going to get hurt."

Her dad sighed and looked over at her mom, who'd come down into the kitchen to see what all the noise was about.

"Why can't she go home?" Mom asked, sounding reluctant. "Doesn't she have a cat flap?"

Jasmine shrugged. "Maybe she's too scared to get past Sam."

"I'll go next door and see if the

Murrays are home. It didn't look like their lights were on, though." Dad went around to the front of the house.

Jasmine cuddled Star, feeling her heart racing inside her fragile body. She was still such a little cat.

Dad came back, shaking his head. "No, they're definitely out."

Jasmine's mom sighed. "Well, maybe we had better hold onto her. Just until Helen and Andy get home. They must have gone out for the evening."

Even though it was late, Jasmine's mom and dad let her stay downstairs with Star—it was a Friday evening, so there was no school the next day. And when Jasmine pointed out that Star probably hadn't eaten, Mom even found a can of tuna for her.

But it got later and later, and Jasmine couldn't stop yawning. Star was curled up fast asleep on her lap on the sofa, and Jasmine's mom shook her head, laughing.

"Go up to bed, Jasmine. And yes, you can take her with you; otherwise, she'll howl herself silly in the kitchen. We'll just have to take her back in the morning."

Jasmine looked up at her in delight. "Really?" She had been trying so hard not to yawn in case Mom sent her off to bed, but she'd never thought they'd let her take Star upstairs, not after what Mom had said last time.

She stood up, draping sleepy little Star over her shoulder like a soft, furry scarf, and crept upstairs. She set Star down on her bed while she took off her robe, then snuggled carefully under the comforter, trying not to disturb her.

Jasmine was just drifting off to sleep when she heard a quiet purring, just next to her ear, as Star burrowed down beside her. Jasmine smiled in her sleep and felt like purring, too.

The next morning Jasmine slept late after her exciting night, and it was nine o'clock when she and Star wandered downstairs. It had been so wonderful waking up and finding a cat curled up next to her!

Star sat on Jasmine's lap and sniffed hopefully at the toast. Jasmine smiled. "I think Star's hungry, Mom!"

Jasmine's mom looked at her worriedly. "I wonder what she usually has for breakfast. I don't want to make her sick with too much tuna."

Jasmine's dad looked over at them. "We should let the Murrays know where she is—they'll be worried about her."

Jasmine sighed. She was enjoying pretending Star was hers, but it looked like the game wouldn't last long.

She was just finishing her toast when the doorbell rang, and her mom went to answer it. Jasmine could hear Mom chatting to someone, and then she came back in with Helen and Andy from next door.

Star gave a delighted little purr and jumped off Jasmine's lap, scampering over to Helen.

"That's not very grateful!" Helen laughed. "Jasmine, your mom says you saved Star from that great big black cat from down the street. Thank you for rescuing her." She shook her head. "She's been wandering off at night quite a bit recently. I know she's just getting bigger and braver, but I wish she wouldn't. Oh, well. Maybe she'll be a bit less daring for a while after her scare."

Star trotted back over and rubbed her head up against Jasmine's robe. She was delighted to see her owners, but she did love Jasmine, too.

Helen gave Jasmine a thoughtful look, watching the way Star was snuggling against her.

While Jasmine said good-bye to Star, the Murrays went to talk to her mom and dad in the hallway.

"Jasmine, do you think you could do us a huge favor?" said Helen as she came back into the kitchen and gathered up Star. "We're going away for three weeks over Christmas, and we haven't quite decided what to do with this little one. Star's such a friendly thing, and we think she'd hate to be boarded, where no one had much time to play with her." She paused. "Would you like to take care of her for us?"

Jasmine's eyes opened wide with delight and she looked hopefully at her mom and dad. To take care of Star, for three whole weeks! She couldn't imagine anything she'd like more.

Chapter Three
A Special Opportunity

Jasmine was counting down the days until the Murrays went away. She and her mom went next door after school one night, so that the Murrays could go through everything Jasmine would need to know. They weren't going on vacation for another few days, but they wanted to get things organized in advance.

Star met them at the door, meowing with delight at the sight of Jasmine.

Helen laughed. "This was such a good idea! I was really worried about Star being miserable at a boarding kennel. Come in."

They sat down at the kitchen table to look at a list that Helen had made of all the things she thought Jasmine would need to know, like the phone number of their vet, just in case.

Mom frowned. "I hope you can manage all this, Jasmine," she said, looking at the part about measuring out Star's special food so she didn't have too much.

"Don't worry, Mom, of course I can," Jasmine told her. "And I'll get up earlier so I can stop in and see Star before school to feed her."

But when they got home, Jasmine couldn't help worrying a little, too. Not about feeding Star and taking care of her; she was sure she could do that. No, she was worried about all the time Star would be on her own in the Murrays' house. She was a cat who loved attention—that's why she came into Jasmine's yard all the time. How would she feel about being alone every night? Now that it was almost December, it was getting really cold. Mom wasn't going to let Jasmine sit out in the yard with Star for very long if it started snowing!

Maybe Mom would let me bring her inside for some of the time, Jasmine wondered to herself. *I'm sure Helen and Andy wouldn't mind....* Oh! Jasmine smiled excitedly. She had just had the most wonderful idea.

What if she took care of Star at her house instead? It would be like having a cat of her very own!

Now all she had to do was persuade Mom and Dad....

"But we don't want a cat in the house, Jasmine," Mom said. "It's all arranged; you'll feed Star next door."

Jasmine nodded. "I know, but it would be so much better if she was here. She's so friendly, Mom; she'd hate being on her own all day. And she'd be company for you while you're working." She looked at her mom hopefully. It wasn't just that she really wanted to have Star stay—she was sure that Mom and Dad would fall in love with Star if they saw more of her. And if Jasmine could take great care of Star and give her back to the Murrays as the world's best-cared-for cat, wouldn't her parents be tempted to let her have a cat of her own? Once they knew how nice it would be to have a cat in the house?

"Pets are a bit messy, Jasmine," Dad explained. "We don't have a cat flap, for starters, so that would be a problem...."

"But we could put a litter box in the corner of the kitchen," Jasmine suggested eagerly. "I bet the Murrays have one, and if not, I'll buy one with my own money."

Mom smiled. "I thought you were saving up for my Christmas present!"

Jasmine grinned at her. "Oh, I bought your present a long time ago, when you let me go Christmas shopping with Laura. Please, Mom," she added. "It's only for three weeks. I promise you won't have to do anything—I'll take care of her all by myself. I'll even do the vacuuming in case Star sheds on the carpet. Oh, pleeease! She'll be so miserable all on her own...."

Mom and Dad exchanged a look. "Well, I suppose we could ask Helen and Andy what they think," Dad said, rather reluctantly.

"Yes!" Jasmine flung her arms around his neck. "This is the best Christmas present ever!"

Star sniffed thoughtfully at the pile of bags in the hallway. What was going on? Her owners seemed to be very excited, and kept running up and down the stairs.

"Oh, Star! I almost put that on top of you. Careful, kitty cat!" Helen picked her up and petted her. "We're going to miss you. But Jasmine will take care of you so well. We'd better get your things together."

Next door, Jasmine was watching the clock anxiously. *It's almost eight o'clock*, she thought. *Oh, I hope they hurry. I really want to spend some time with Star before we have to go to school!*

"There's the doorbell!" Jasmine exclaimed. She leaped up from her chair and rushed to answer it.

Ten minutes later, the Murrays were on their way to the airport, and Jasmine was showing Star where her bowls and litter box were. It was so exciting watching her sniffing around the kitchen, her whiskers twitching delicately as she investigated all the interesting corners. Jasmine picked her up and petted her lovingly, and Star rubbed her ears against Jasmine's cheek.

"Come and see my bedroom," Jasmine

told her. She laughed. "You can read my cat books while I'm at school."

"Oh, I thought we'd keep her in the kitchen for now," Mom said.

"But she'd hate that, Mom! It'll be all right. Mrs. Murray said she's good about using a litter box—she won't make a mess."

Mom frowned. "Are you sure? Won't she be worried about being in a new place?"

Jasmine looked down at Star, who was purring in her arms. "She doesn't look very worried…."

Mom nodded, a little reluctantly. "I suppose not. Come on, then. We need to get to school."

Jasmine sighed. "I hope she won't be lonely without me…," she muttered.

Star sat in the middle of Jasmine's bed. She was confused. She'd been scolded for being in this house before, she remembered. But she was definitely supposed to be here now, because her owners had brought her over that morning, and they'd brought her bowls and her bed, too. Her bed was downstairs in the kitchen, but Jasmine's was nicer.

Star sniffed. The bed smelled like Jasmine, which was comforting. She had stayed in the kitchen for a while, but Jasmine's mom kept watching her and looking worried, and it had made Star feel worried, too. Then Jasmine's mom had gone into another room, and she hadn't liked it when Star tried to play with the wires on her computer. Helen always laughed when she did that.

Star had wondered if she'd done something wrong, if her owners didn't want her anymore, but they hadn't seemed angry. They'd held her and petted her and made a big deal over her. Star was sure they were coming back. And meanwhile she had Jasmine, who was almost as good. Star stretched out her front paws, yawned, and curled up to sleep. She hoped Jasmine would come home soon.

"Oh, Jasmine, she's so pretty! You're so lucky!" Jasmine's friend Laura had come home from school with her to see Star.

The girls had gone straight upstairs and found the kitten snoozing on Jasmine's bed. She was lying on her back with her paws folded on her soft cream and brown tummy, making a funny little whistling noise—a very small cat's snore.

Laura was only whispering, but Star opened one eye thoughtfully, and then bounced up, purring delightedly at Jasmine. She was back!

"Isn't she beautiful?" Jasmine said proudly. Then she sighed. "It's almost like having a cat of my own."

Laura nodded. "Three weeks is a long time. Oh, I wish someone wanted me to cat-sit! I'm sure your parents will get to like her—how can they resist! You never know—then they might let you have your own cat."

Jasmine nodded, sitting down on the bed and hugging Star close. "That's what I'm really hoping, but I'm not sure it'll work. Mom was really complaining this morning about not wanting Star to get into her office and mess up her paperwork. She wanted to keep her in the kitchen all day, but I convinced her that it wouldn't be fair. I think they only let me take care of

Star because they wanted to help out the people next door. Neither of them is fond of the idea of having pets. They've said I can have a gerbil or a hamster, but I'd much, much rather have a cat."

Laura and Jasmine looked down at Star. She was purring blissfully to herself as Jasmine petted her, in just the right itchy spot down her spine. She looked up at them, then nudged Jasmine's chin lovingly. Laura and Jasmine both sighed. Who wouldn't want such a beautiful cat?

During the next week, Jasmine wondered if Star had been listening to what she and Laura had said. She seemed to be doing everything she could to charm Jasmine's parents. Maybe it was because Star felt lonely during the day while Jasmine was at school, or maybe it was just that she loved being around people, but she put on her best manners.

On Monday afternoon, Jasmine rushed home from school and let herself in, eager to see Star. But today Star didn't come to say hello.

After looking in the kitchen and her bedroom, Jasmine went to her mom's office to see if she knew where the cat was. She put her head around the office door and found Star and her mom, watching the gleams of rainbow light from the glass prism her mom had hanging in the window. Her mom was laughing as Star leaped around the room, chasing the colored flashes on the wall.

"Aren't you supposed to be working?" she asked her mom sternly.

Mom looked guilty. "Yes. But Star came in, and she seemed to want attention. She's so funny, Jasmine—and so athletic. Look at her jumping!"

Star looked up at Jasmine lovingly, and then meowed hopefully at Jasmine's mom.

"Oh, do you want me to swing it for you again?" Mom reached up to tap the prism, sending the rainbows all around the wall again, and Star was off in a crazy cat dance, leaping and batting at the pretty lights.

Jasmine huffed and went to get herself a drink. It wasn't that she didn't like her mom getting along with Star—after all, it was exactly what she'd wanted! But Jasmine did feel a tiny bit jealous. *She* played with Star. She and Laura had stopped by the pet store on the way home, and she'd bought a jingly ball for her. But Mom's rainbow lights looked much more exciting!

Dad took a bit longer to fall for Star. He didn't really spend much time with her, and he got very upset when he discovered she'd slept on his favorite sweater and left it covered in brown fur. But on Sunday morning, Jasmine came downstairs and found Dad reading the newspaper, and Star sitting on the kitchen table (which she wasn't allowed to do). She was batting at the back of the paper. Every time she did it, Dad would twitch the paper straight, and Star would wait a few seconds and whack it again with her paw.

Jasmine watched her do it three more times before Dad snorted with laughter and folded up the paper. Star jumped delicately onto his lap and gazed up at him with big green eyes.

Jasmine's dad looked down at her, as though he wasn't quite sure what he was supposed to do now. He put out a cautious hand and petted her, very lightly down her back. Then he looked up at Jasmine, as if he thought she might tell him he'd done it wrong.

Jasmine sighed and shook her head, smiling. Star had managed it again. She'd even won Dad over!

Dad petted Star again, more confidently this time. "This cat," he told Jasmine as she got herself a bowl of cereal, "has a real sense of humor." He reached over and grabbed a packet of cat treats that had been left on the counter. Star sat up on his lap, her tail twitching eagerly, and he fed her three, one after the other. She crunched them up quickly, with her eyes closed in delight.

"Not too many, Dad." Jasmine pointed at him with her cereal spoon. "She'll get too big. In fact...," Jasmine looked worriedly at Star's silky tummy. Was it her imagination, or was it larger than before? "She's getting really round, Dad, now that I look at her! I bet Mom's been feeding her tons of treats while I'm at school."

Jasmine didn't mention the number of times she'd saved a little bit of chicken or turkey to feed to Star as an extra-special treat, but she couldn't help feeling a bit guilty. She'd just wanted to make Star happy—and it was so sweet the way she nibbled the scraps off her fingers.

Jasmine's mom came downstairs and frowned when Jasmine asked her about the treats. "Well, I've given her some. But not that many, Jasmine. I wouldn't have thought it would be enough to make her get too big." She eyed Star thoughtfully as she sat on Dad's lap and washed her ears. "Hmmm. She is looking a bit rounder, you're right. Oh, dear. I don't know much about cats, but I'm sure it isn't healthy for her to be too large."

"I'll try and get her to do some more running around," Jasmine said, wondering what the Murrays would say if they came home and found they had a cat larger than when they had left.

Star seemed to be able to tell that Jasmine was worried. She stopped washing and gazed lovingly at her from Dad's lap. Then she sat up on her hind legs with her front paws in the air, as though she was begging to be picked up. It was so funny Jasmine choked on her mouthful of cereal.

Dad grinned. "You see? She definitely has a sense of humor!"

Chapter Four
The Exercise Plan

Jasmine started Star's exercise routine the next day when she got home from school. They had decorated the Christmas tree over the weekend, and Star had been fascinated by it. The moment Jasmine and her mom went into the kitchen for a drink, Star had climbed up it, then got stuck near the top, wailing frantically as she wobbled on a branch. Jasmine had had to rescue her, and ever since then Star had looked at the tree with great suspicion.

But Star had loved playing with the sparkly ribbon, rolling over and over and chewing it. Jasmine wasn't sure how people got cute photos of cats wearing ribbon on their collars. Star would have eaten it before anyone had a chance to get a camera out. So ribbon seemed to be a good idea for getting Star to jump around. It was the end of school in a couple of days. She could do a lot more exercising with Star when it was the Christmas holidays. She was really looking forward to being at home and being able to play with Star all the time.

Jasmine carefully unwound a bit of sparkly ribbon from around the back of the tree, where no one would really notice it was gone. She crouched down in front of Star, holding the sparkly strand. It shimmered and twinkled, almost as if it were alive, and Star's tail flicked back and forth as she watched it. She stuck out a paw, and Jasmine twitched the ribbon away so that Star missed it. The cat sprang forward, paws batting here and there, dancing and springing as Jasmine giggled and waved the ribbon for her. At one point Jasmine was sure that Star leaped at least a couple of feet off the ground in a truly amazing jump.

Eventually, Jasmine gave up as she was worn out, although Star was still full of energy. She lay on her back, tugging at the ribbon with her paws and trying to shred it.

"Well, that certainly should have worked off a few cat treats," Mom said from the doorway where she'd been watching. "But if you do it again tomorrow, can you use string instead? We won't have any ribbon left at this rate."

Jasmine looked at the sparkly bits all over the floor. "Sorry, Mom. I didn't know she'd tear it up like that. I was going to put it back on the tree."

They looked at each other, and then down at the sparkly pieces that were all that was left of the ribbon.

"Maybe not...," Jasmine said, giggling, as Star abandoned the ribbon, suddenly tired out, and climbed exhaustedly into her lap. She stretched herself out over Jasmine's legs and went completely floppy, making just a very faint, wheezy purr, as though it was all she had the strength for.

Luckily, the cat dancing game worked almost as well with string, especially when Jasmine invented a fun new cat toy by tying some of the feathers from a craft set she had onto the string to make it more exciting. They had a great game with it after school on Thursday afternoon. Laura was there, too, to celebrate the start of the Christmas holidays. Mom had gotten them the ingredients to make some snowmen cookies, which Jasmine had seen in a magazine, and they sat in the kitchen taking turns licking the bowl while the cookies baked. Laura offered a teensy bit of cookie batter to Star, who was sitting next to her on a chair, purring loudly. Jasmine laughed as Star eagerly licked Laura's fingers.

"Don't give her any more." Jasmine said. "Even with all the exercise she's been getting, she's still got that little round tummy. In fact, it seems bigger! But I know we're not overfeeding her. I've checked the instructions on the cat food really carefully." She sighed. "I wonder if she's helping herself to food at another cat's house. I wouldn't put it past her. She's so cute that she can get away with anything."

Laura nodded. "I can't believe she won over your mom and dad, after all you said about them not liking cats."

Jasmine smiled. "It's amazing. I've loved taking care of Star so much, and I'm really going to miss her when the Murrays get back. I know she'll only be next door, but she won't be sleeping on my bed every night. I've been hoping Star might have charmed Mom and Dad enough that they'd let me have a cat of my own...."

"You really think they will?" said Laura excitedly.

Jasmine reached over and tickled Star lovingly under her chin. "I'm not sure.... If the Murrays come home and say Star's gotten bigger because we've been overfeeding her, I won't have a chance!"

"But I'm sure the Murrays will see how happy Star is and how well you've taken care of her. You really love her, and she adores you—you can tell she does." Laura licked her spoon. "You wouldn't mind having a cat that wasn't Star, though?"

Jasmine looked thoughtful. "It would be weird," she admitted. "Star's so special. But I know she isn't mine. I've always known that. And you haven't seen her with Mr. and Mrs. Murray from next door. She's clearly their cat. I mean, she likes me, but it isn't quite the same." She grinned at Laura. "I need Star number two!"

Jasmine woke up the next morning feeling so happy. At first she couldn't remember why, but then she realized it was the first full day of Christmas vacation, and she had a busy day of making Christmas cards and wrapping presents planned. The weather forecast had said there would be snow today, too, lots of it. It sounded as though it was going to be a real white Christmas. Jasmine smiled to herself, imagining Star chasing snowflakes, batting at them with her little paws.

She yawned and sat up, ready to pet Star. But she wasn't there. Surprised, Jasmine looked under her comforter in case she had crept underneath. She did that sometimes. No Star. She wasn't hiding in Jasmine's closet, under the bed, or on her beanbag chair, either.

Jasmine threw on her robe and went downstairs, feeling worried. Star was always there when she woke up! Or sometimes she got sick of waiting and rubbed around Jasmine's face until she woke up. But she'd never gone downstairs without Jasmine before.

She found Star in the kitchen, meowing at her mom, who was scooping cat food into her bowl. She didn't even look at Jasmine, just danced and hopped around Mom's legs until she put the bowl down.

"She seems hungry this morning!" Mom commented.

"Mmm." Jasmine didn't want to say anything. She felt a bit silly, as if she was making a big deal over nothing.

But it was the same all day. Star didn't seem to want to play. She ignored the string and feathers toy when Jasmine waved it in front of her nose, and she didn't seem interested in wrapping presents at all. She went and slept on the couch for the entire afternoon, and

Jasmine felt really lonely. It was silly, because she'd only been taking care of Star for a couple of weeks—but now that Star didn't want to be with her, it felt awful.

Jasmine watched Star anxiously as she munched on her snack. It was the only time Star had been friendly all day— when she wanted Jasmine to feed her.

"She's starving again," Mom commented, smiling as she watched Star gobbling her food.

Jasmine nodded. "Mom, do you think Star is all right?" she asked worriedly. "She hasn't been very friendly today, not like she usually is. And she slept all afternoon!"

Mom looked at her in surprise. "Well, I don't think she's sick, not the way she's eating!"

Jasmine sighed. "I guess not. Maybe I've been making a big deal over her too much."

Mom gave her a hug. "Don't worry. Cats have moods just like people. Maybe Star just feels like having some time to herself today."

Star licked all the way around her food bowl and looked at it for a moment in case it magically refilled itself. Then she turned around and walked out of the kitchen without even looking at Jasmine.

Chapter Five
Feeling Strange

Star was feeling strange. She didn't know why, but things felt different. She knew she needed to find somewhere quiet and warm, and just curl up and be on her own for a while. But no one seemed to want her to do that!

Star loved Jasmine, and usually she adored all the attention and cuddling she got at Jasmine's house, but not right now. After breakfast that morning, she set off determined to find herself a quiet little nest.

But everywhere in the house seemed busy, and noisy, and full of people—which, considering only Jasmine and her mom were there, was strange. Grumpily, Star wandered back into the kitchen to see if there was any more food in her bowl. She was so hungry at the moment! Then she spotted the perfect place....

Jasmine's mom had been looking for the red tablecloth she liked to use for Christmas lunch, and she'd left a drawer in the big kitchen cupboard half open. Star peered into it interestedly. It was full of hand towels and tablecloths. Warm, soft, clean things that would be perfect to snuggle up and snooze on. Star wondered why she had never noticed it before—it was just right! She stepped in and curled up at the back of the drawer, yawning and closing her eyes.

Some time later, Star woke up to find herself in complete darkness. She opened her eyes very wide, her heart thudding, unable to figure out where she was. Then she remembered. Her soft, cozy nest. What had happened to it? Why had it gotten dark? She edged forward to where the opening had been and pawed at the wooden walls. She was shut in a tight, dark box! Panicking, Star scratched and scuffled at the front of the drawer, and meowed frantically.

Jasmine and her mom were making cards at the kitchen table. "That sounds like Star," said Jasmine. "I was wondering where she was. She's shut in somewhere, Mom!"

"I don't understand," Jasmine's mom muttered, opening cupboards. "Where can she be? Oh! Oh, dear, the drawer!"

Star blinked and cowered as her nest moved sharply, bumping her head against the top of the drawer. She was pulled out into the light, huddling against the towels.

"Oh, poor Star...." Jasmine lifted her out, and Star snuggled gratefully against her.

"What on earth was she doing in there?" Jasmine's mom asked, sounding a bit guilty—she had been the one who shut Star in.

"I suppose she was just looking for somewhere cozy to sleep," Jasmine suggested. "It wasn't your fault, Mom; you couldn't have known she was there." She petted Star's head gently. "I know we're cutting back, but I think she really deserves a cat treat!"

Mom and Jasmine went back to card-making, and Star played half-heartedly with some pencils, but she couldn't really enjoy the game. She was still feeling the need to find herself a quiet place to rest, and she sneaked away to go searching again. This time she found a space under the stairs. It was quiet and dark, and it didn't have a door that anyone could close on her by accident. There were a lot of odd things stored under there: boots, roller skates, and a big basket full of gloves and scarves and hats. Star scrambled up the side and turned around several times, purring throatily. This was just right. She would stay here.

But it didn't last. Star was sleeping peacefully when she felt her hiding place shudder as Jasmine raced up the stairs over her head, calling for her. And then Jasmine's mom hauled out the vacuum cleaner, which was right next to her basket bed.

"Oh, Star, I didn't see you. She's down here, Jasmine!" Mom called. And Jasmine came dashing down the stairs again, thud, thump, thud, and picked Star up to cuddle her.

Star was still half-asleep, and she was grumpy. She didn't want to be picked up. She wanted to be left alone. Angrily, she gave a loud hiss, lashed out with her claws, and scratched Jasmine's arm.

Jasmine was so surprised that she yelled and dropped Star, who hissed and shot into the kitchen. There she yowled at Jasmine's mom until she opened the back door.

Jasmine clutched her arm, which was oozing a few spots of blood. She entered the kitchen just in time to see Star's gray and brown striped tail disappearing around the back door. Then she sat down at the kitchen table and cried. Star had scratched her—and then Jasmine had scared her so much by shouting that she'd run away!

Star stayed out in the yard until it got dark, hiding under a clump of bushes.

She was shivering from the cold and knew she couldn't stay out all night. But she'd spent a long time trying to figure out where she could go and hadn't found anywhere good. Everywhere was too busy, too full of people.

She crept out from under her bush and sneaked over to the hole under the fence. She didn't quite have the energy to climb over the fence right now. She dug a little with her claws, widening the hole, then squeezed herself underneath. She had been back to her own yard quite a lot while she was staying at Jasmine's house, trying to make sure all the local cats knew it was still hers. Maybe she could go and make a nest in the bushes…. She shivered again. No, it was much too cold, colder than she'd ever felt it, and the ground was frozen hard. She needed somewhere really warm.

Her house! Of course. She had been back a few times since she'd been staying with Jasmine to see if the Murrays had come back, but it felt strange and empty. Now the quiet house felt like just what she needed.

Eagerly, Star scurried over to the door and nosed at her cat flap, squeezing herself in.

It was so quiet. No one around. Very warm, or at least warmer than the bushes. Perfect. She looked around the kitchen thoughtfully, trying to think of a good place to go.

After her experience with drawers at Jasmine's house, she didn't want anywhere too small and tight. Star set off upstairs and tried all the beds, but they weren't right, either—too out in the open. At last, in the smaller bedroom, she found the linen closet. The door was shut, but it only had a light catch, and the door itself was made of wooden slats that were perfect for claws to hook between.

Star pulled it open and crept in, sniffing delightedly at the clean, fresh smell. The floor was covered in a pile of old towels, and she curled up on them, closing her eyes peacefully. She was home. Just in time.

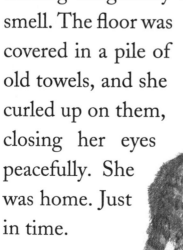

Chapter Six
The Missing Kitten

It was almost bedtime. By now Jasmine was panicking. She couldn't find Star anywhere. She'd even checked the kitchen cupboard drawer, just in case.

"She's run away because I shouted at her!" Jasmine wailed. "It's all my fault!"

"She's probably just out exploring," Jasmine's mom suggested, trying to calm her down. "You know she likes to go off and sniff around in those bushes next door."

Jasmine bolted out into the dark yard, without even putting on her coat, and raced down to the end. She climbed up her mom's rock garden—which she definitely wasn't allowed to do—and peered over at the end of the Murrays' yard. A few tiny snowflakes drifted gently past her nose, and she shivered.

"Star! Star! Here, kitty, kitty...." She tried again and again, but no little stripy cat appeared out of the trailing branches, looking up at her lovingly.

Jasmine wandered sadly back up the yard. She looked so unhappy that her mom didn't bother scolding her.

"She isn't there."

"You don't know that, Jasmine. She

might just not want to come out."

"But why?" Jasmine cried. "Why doesn't she want to play anymore? What have I done to make her not like me? I was supposed to be taking care of her! She used to like me, I know she did, but she even scratched me! She's never done that before."

She slumped down in a kitchen chair, and her mom sat down next to her. "Jasmine, it isn't your fault. You've taken care of her really well. Cats are like that sometimes. They can get touchy and grumpy, just like people can. She's probably stalking blackbirds in a yard a few doors down. I'm sure she'll be back soon."

Jasmine gave her a disbelieving look. "It's starting to snow out there, Mom!

It's freezing! Star wouldn't want to stay out in this weather—she likes being warm." Jasmine looked over at Star's bowl, which was full of food. "She hasn't even come back for her food, and she must be really hungry by now. Oh, what if she doesn't come back? What are we going to do? How will we tell the Murrays?"

Mom thought for a moment, then smiled. "Do you know what I think? I think that Star has probably gone back home!"

Jasmine's mouth opened, then she grinned back at her mom. "Of course she has!" She hugged her around the waist lovingly. "Oh, Mom, you're so clever! Why didn't I think of that?"

The house felt strange, cold and very quiet. Jasmine couldn't help feeling guilty, as though she was trespassing. She was glad Mom had come with her.

She had hoped that Star would come out to meet her as soon as she opened the door, but no little stripy cat appeared, meowing in welcome. Then Jasmine had an awful thought—what if Star had accidentally gotten herself shut in somewhere like she had earlier? That was only because Mom had shut the drawer, of course, but Star could easily have gotten herself trapped if a door had swung closed. And no one had been here to let her out! Jasmine ran through the house, calling and calling for Star, until her voice hurt and Mom told her gently to stop.

Tucked away inside the warm linen closet, Star could hear Jasmine calling her name. She was tempted to meow and let Jasmine know where she was— she missed her soft petting, the loving whispers, and the delicious treats Jasmine always had for her. But for now, she needed to be alone. She wasn't ready quite yet. Soon.

Mom had her arm around Jasmine as they walked back home. "She'll turn up," she told her, trying to sound encouraging. "You know Mrs. Murray said she'd been wandering a bit."

"Did you find her?" Dad opened the front door as they came down the path.

Jasmine shook her head sadly, and Dad gave her a hug. "I'll help you look for her tomorrow," he promised. But he gave his wife a worried frown over Jasmine's head.

"I don't think we'll ever find her!" Jasmine wailed.

"Oh, sweetheart, you're getting way ahead of yourself! If she isn't back in the morning, then we'll go and look for her. But she will be. You'll see."

Just before Jasmine went to bed that night, she went to close her bedroom curtains and peered out at the night-filled yard. There were deep shadows everywhere, and it looked frightening. Jasmine hated to think of Star out there somewhere all on her own. Last time Star had been out at night, Jasmine had rescued her. But now she wasn't even sure Star would want to be rescued. Or at least not by her.

"If only I hadn't shouted at her like that," she whispered miserably to her reflection in the window.

Suddenly the dark sky filled with thick snowflakes, and Jasmine watched sadly as they began to cover the yard in frozen whiteness.

Chapter Seven
A Magical Surprise

To: Jasmine
From: Mrs. Murray
Subject: Hello!

We're having a wonderful time. Saw a newspaper
and can't believe it's snowing back at home, and
we're sunbathing and swimming in the ocean here!
Hope you're really enjoying it, though—it's the
first time Star has seen snow. Make a snowman
for us!
Love from Mr. and Mrs. Murray

P.S. Merry Christmas! Go next door and look in the
cupboard under the sink. There's a little present
for you and one for Star—her favorite salmon
treats!

A fat tear splashed onto the keyboard. It was snowing still, just in time for a white Christmas, the first one in years. Everyone was really excited about it, but Jasmine couldn't care less. Laura had invited her to come over and build an igloo in her yard, but Jasmine couldn't face it. She just kept imagining poor Star, shivering in the middle of a snowstorm, icicles hanging off her whiskers. It was the worst Christmas ever. She couldn't even feel excited about presents.

"Do you think we should call and tell them she's gone?" Jasmine asked her mom sadly. The Murrays' email said they'd gotten her a present to say thank you for taking care of Star so well.... She felt so miserably guilty.

"They left the number of their hotel, didn't they?"

"Yes, they did," said Mom. "But Star's only been gone one night, and we don't want to ruin their vacation. There's nothing they could do. I'm sure she'll be back by the time they fly home in a few days anyway."

Jasmine nodded. She supposed Mom was right. It would only make the Murrays really sad, and there was a chance she might still find her....

She'd spent the morning going up and down the street with Dad, peering under bushes and looking behind walls. Jasmine had even asked everyone she knew in the street to look in their sheds and garages, and tell their neighbors. Feeling helpless, she went to put on her coat. She didn't really think she'd find Star now, but she couldn't give up. It was Christmas Eve tomorrow. How could she leave Star lost out in the snow at Christmas?

"Are you going out again?" her mom asked worriedly. "Honestly, Jasmine, you'll freeze! Do you want me to come?"

Jasmine shook her head. "It's okay. Maybe later."

She was plodding up the pavement through the snow, which was already turning gray and slushy, when she had a thought. The Murrays' email had said they'd left some of Star's favorite salmon cat treats, and Jasmine knew she really did love those. She turned into the most adoring little cat ever when you were about to open a packet, weaving around your legs, meowing loudly. Maybe if Star was hiding in one of the yards somewhere—and that was what Jasmine was hoping—she'd come back if she smelled those yummy salmon treats....

Jasmine dashed back home to get the Murrays' keys and headed down the path next door.

I shouldn't be opening Star's present before Christmas, Jasmine thought to herself as she ripped open the shiny paper, *but this is an emergency*.

She was just tearing at the foil pouch with her nails when she heard it. A loud piercing, demanding, very squeaky meow. From upstairs.

Star was here!

Although that didn't sound quite like

Star. Could another cat have gotten in?

Jasmine crept up the stairs, feeling half-hopeful, half-scared. She wasn't quite sure what to expect—even if it was Star up there, would she be happy to see her? She'd been so grumpy the day she disappeared.

The strange meowing continued as Jasmine reached the landing. She opened one of the bedroom doors and peered around. It seemed empty. But then the squeaky meow came again, and she realized that there was another door, over in the corner, almost hidden by the dresser. And it was very slightly open.

"Star?" Jasmine whispered nervously.

There was a moment's silence, and then Jasmine heard a very familiar purr. Star! It was definitely her, and she was purring as a welcome. Jasmine wanted to race across the room and hug her, but she told herself to be calm and not get too excited. It was probably her enthusiasm that had made Star leave in the first place. She walked quietly

over to the linen closet and very gently
opened the door.

There was Star, lying curled on a pile
of towels and purring delightedly at
Jasmine.

And snuggled up next
to her were two tiny
newborn kittens.

Chapter Eight
A Sparkly Christmas

Star stared up at Jasmine, purring proudly. She was very pleased that Jasmine had found her—she wanted to show off her beautiful babies. And she was absolutely starving—she hadn't eaten for an entire day now, and she'd been feeding her kittens, too. She had thought about going to find Jasmine, and some food, but she hadn't wanted to leave her kittens—she knew they needed her. She had hoped and hoped that Jasmine would come, and now she had. She meowed at Jasmine, who seemed to be holding a food packet.

Jasmine crouched down and poured some salmon treats out into her hand. "Oh, you must be starving, poor Star," she whispered, gently scattering them in front of Star's nose, without getting too close to the kittens. She didn't want to upset Star.

Luckily, Star didn't seem to mind being found, but Jasmine knew she would be very protective of her little ones.

She sat back on her heels, a little ways away from the closet, and laughed to herself. "I thought I'd been feeding you too much, Star! I thought you were just getting a little plump, but you were going to have kittens!"

Star licked her kittens' heads fondly with her own little pink tongue. Jasmine's eyes filled with tears. It was so grown up, such a mother cat thing to do, and Star was only a baby herself, really too young to have kittens.

"But I guess you didn't know you were too young," Jasmine muttered. "Wow. Mr. and Mrs. Murray have three cats now; they're so lucky!" She looked admiringly at the kittens. They were about as long as two of her fingers. One of them was a beautifully striped orange cat, and the other looked like a baby Star—only with slightly more gray in her tabby fur. Their eyes were closed, and their ears were almost invisible, still tucked against their heads.

Star gave her a slightly anxious look, and Jasmine smiled. "They're beautiful. Beautiful kittens." She couldn't tell if they were boys or girls. Then she frowned slightly. She hoped Star was okay. Was there anything she should do for her? Did she need to go to a vet?

Jasmine carefully backed away from the closet, not wanting to startle Star or the kittens—although they were fast asleep and didn't look like much could disturb them right now. "I'll be back soon," she whispered. "And I'll bring you some more food and water, and a litter box."

Jasmine raced downstairs and back to her own house. "Mom! Mom!" she called excitedly.

Her mom rushed out of the kitchen. "Have you found her? Oh, you have, haven't you? Great job, Jasmine!" She peered over Jasmine's shoulder, expecting to see Star following her. "But where is she?"

Jasmine beamed and hugged her. She'd almost forgotten how miserable and frightened she had been about losing Star, and now an incredible relief flooded over her in waves. She needed to hold onto someone. "You're not going to believe it," she said into her mom's shoulder.

"What? Has she been somewhere really obvious all the time? What's happened?"

"She's in the linen closet next door." Jasmine grinned at her. "And she's had kittens!"

"No!" Jasmine's mom gasped. "You mean it? Star has? How could we not have noticed that she was pregnant?"

Jasmine laughed. "I don't know! I guess we just thought she was too young. There are only two kittens, so I guess that's why she wasn't really that big. We did think she was getting big, didn't we? I need to go and find all my cat books, Mom. I need to know what we should do!"

Jasmine was very careful not to upset Star by making a big deal over her and the kittens too much. She knew now that Star had been grumpy because she was about to have the kittens, and her cat instincts were telling her that she needed to hide somewhere safe. But she was pretty sure that Star would still be wary about anyone getting too close. So she left kitten food—her books said that was what Star needed right now, as it was high in energy—and water bowls and a litter box just outside the closet. She then strictly rationed herself to a five-minute visit every couple of hours. Her mom had called the vet, whose number the Murrays had left. The receptionist had said that it sounded like Star was doing wonderfully all by herself, but to call if there were any problems.

It had gone from being the worst Christmas Jasmine could have imagined to the absolute best. She spent the time between her visits to Star and the kittens looking up kitten care on the computer and nibbling her nails, wishing the time would go faster.

"I wish we could pet the kittens," she said to her mom the next morning. "I know we shouldn't, because they're too little, but they look so soft and cuddly."

"Mmm." Jasmine's mom wasn't listening, as she was trying to figure out exactly how long to cook the Christmas turkey for the next day. "Do you think we should have sweet potatoes, Jasmine? I can't remember if you like them."

"I don't," Jasmine said. "Ooh, Mom, we'll have to take Star some Christmas dinner tomorrow. Just a little bit. Please?"

Mom shook her head, laughing. "The poor Murrays, coming home to find a cat eating Christmas dinner in their linen closet!"

Jasmine smiled. "They won't mind," she said. She knew how much the Murrays adored Star. "They'll be so excited about the kittens. It's going to be such a wonderful surprise. They're so lucky, coming back to three cats instead of one!"

Mom looked thoughtful. "I don't know. Having three cats is a lot, all at once. But I'm sure they'll be able to find good homes for the kittens."

Jasmine blinked back sudden tears. She hadn't thought that the Murrays might not keep the kittens—she'd been really looking forward to having three cats next door now! She didn't notice that Mom was watching her, a strange, thoughtful expression on her face.

"I'll just go and check on them all," Jasmine muttered. "I'll take Star some more of that special cat milk." Mom had made an emergency trip to the pet store yesterday to buy some kitten food and some milk that was made to be safe for cats' stomachs.

She sat by the linen closet door watching Star, who was looking down at her feeding babies with a very contented look on her face.

"Oh, Star, I hope the Murrays will keep them," Jasmine said. "I don't want you to lose your kittens!"

But Star wasn't listening. She was gently licking the orange kitten's ears, as if making sure they were perfectly clean was the most important thing in the world.

Jasmine woke up very early on Christmas morning. She smiled delightedly as she felt the heavy weight of her stocking next to her feet and sat up to see if she could feel what was in it.

Then she frowned. Was that meowing? Jasmine turned on her bedside light and listened again. Star was safe next door, and she'd checked on her last thing the night before, but—yes, there it was again. Jasmine ran downstairs and unlocked the back door to find Star standing there, with the little tabby kitten held in her mouth. Star dashed inside—*she's probably worried about the kitten catching cold*, Jasmine thought, looking out at the yard as she closed the door. There had been another snowfall during the night, and the grass was covered in a fresh white layer, which looked weird

117

and blue-gray in the darkness.

"Where are you going, Star?" she asked, following the little cat as she trotted through the dark hallway. She flinched as Star started to climb the stairs, determinedly heaving the kitten up each step. Jasmine desperately wanted to help, but she wasn't sure if Star would let her.

Eventually, they reached the landing, and Star headed for Jasmine's bedroom, where she stared meaningfully at the wardrobe.

"Oh!" Jasmine laughed. "You want to have your bed in my wardrobe?" she asked delightedly. She opened the door at once and quickly pulled out her sneakers, then fluffed an old fleece blanket into a comfy nest for Star and the kittens.

Star scrambled in and dropped the kitten gently on the blanket, where it wriggled and made a faint, squeaky little meow. Then Star trotted off to go and get the other kitten.

By lunchtime, Star was well settled, with her food bowls next to the wardrobe. Mom had brought her a few extra morsels of turkey, and Jasmine had even hung some sparkly ribbon over the wardrobe door to make it look Christmassy.

Jasmine had wondered if she might have to go and sleep on the couch, but Star didn't seem to mind her being there—so Jasmine was able to watch her and the kittens a lot more. They were so cute. She was sure that the little tabby one was going to open its eyes soon. They were both beautiful, of course, but the tabby baby was so much like Star, Jasmine couldn't help loving it most of all. She was almost sure it was a girl kitten, because it looked so much like its mom.

It was a strange Christmas Day, but peeking in at the sleeping kittens, Jasmine thought it was the best ever.

Two days later, the Murrays arrived home. They hurried next door to Jasmine's house as soon as they'd dropped off their bags.

Jasmine answered the door, hugging her secret to herself.

"Come and see!" she told them.

"Is Star asleep on your bed?" Mrs. Murry asked as they followed Jasmine upstairs.

"Not quite," Jasmine said mysteriously. She led them into her room and stood back so they could see the scene in her wardrobe.

Star seemed to know she had visitors. She was posed like a queen, and Jasmine was sure she was eyeing the kittens anxiously to make sure they were looking beautiful, too.

"Oh my goodness!" Mrs. Murray crouched down to look. "I had no idea she was pregnant!"

"Neither did we," Jasmine explained. "She started acting a little strangely, and then she disappeared, and…. We wondered if it was because she was really missing you. But actually she was having babies in your linen closet! Mom cleaned it up," she added.

"Clever little Star…," Mrs. Murray said, and Mr. Murray shook his head in amazement. "Talk about keeping it quiet. So now we've got three cats!"

"You're so lucky," Jasmine sighed, and Mrs. Murray looked at her thoughtfully. Leaving Jasmine to tell Mr. Murray the entire story right from the beginning, she beckoned Jasmine's mom out of the room.

They came back a couple of minutes later, just as Jasmine was describing Star arriving at the back door on Christmas morning.

"Your mom agreed that we'd better let them all stay here for the moment. Star probably won't want to be moved," Mrs. Murray said. "As long as you don't mind sharing your bedroom, that is."

"Of course not!" said Jasmine. "What will you do when the kittens are bigger?" she asked. "Will you keep them all?" She wasn't sure that she wanted to know the answer.

"Well, three cats is a lot...," Mrs. Murray said, smiling at Jasmine's mom. "I really love the little orange one—I have a feeling he takes after Tiger, that handsome orange cat down the street."

Jasmine gulped. They didn't want the tabby kitten! She couldn't bear the idea of her special little Christmas kitten being unwanted. It was so unfair.

She almost didn't hear Mrs. Murray as she went on, "But I have an idea. One way that she could have her own home and stay close to her mom."

Jasmine looked up, her eyes full of hope. "You mean...."

Mrs. Murray grinned at her. "Why not?"

Jasmine looked over at her parents. There was no way Mom and Dad would let her. Was there?

Mom smiled. "Would you like to keep her, Jasmine? You know your dad and I have never really wanted to have a cat, but Star won me over. She's so sweet. Your dad really took to having a cat, too—he was so upset when Star was missing. I'd been wondering whether we could keep one of the kittens even before Mrs. Murray asked me," Mom went on. "You took care of Star so well. Dad and I are really proud of you."

"And as the kitten practically started her life in your wardrobe, I don't really think we could say no!" Dad laughed.

Jasmine looked down at the little silvery kitten with new eyes. She could be hers! Star gazed at her lovingly as though she approved of the idea, too.

"What will you name her, Jasmine?" Mom asked.

Jasmine thought for a moment. Something Christmassy. Then she smiled, remembering Star's favorite game. "Sparkles," she said, reaching out, very gently, to pet her new cat.

HOLLY WEBB

Holly Webb started out as a children's book editor, and wrote her first series for the publisher she worked for. She has been writing ever since, with more than 100 books to her name. Holly lives in England with her husband, three young sons, and several cats who are always nosing around when she is trying to type on her laptop.

For more information
about Holly Webb visit:

www.holly-webb.com
www.tigertalesbooks.com